PUFFIN BOOKS

MR MAJEIKA AND THE
HAUNTED HOTEL

Humphrey Carpenter (1946–2005), the author and creator of *Mr Majeika*, was born and educated in Oxford. He went to a school called the Dragon School where exciting things often happened and there were some very odd teachers – you could even call it magical! He became a full-time writer in 1975 and was the author of many award-winning biographies. As well as the *Mr Majeika* titles, his children's books also included *Shakespeare Without the Boring Bits* and *More Shakespeare Without the Boring Bits*. He wrote plays for radio and theatre and founded the children's drama group The Mushy Pea Theatre Company. He played the tuba, double bass, bass saxophone and keyboard.

Humphrey once said, "The nice thing about being a writer is that you can make magic happen without learning tricks. Words are the only tricks you need. I can write: 'He floated up to the ceiling, and a baby rabbit came out of his pocket, grew wings, and flew away.' And you will believe that it really happened! That's magic, isn't it?

HUMPHREY CARPENTER

Mr Majeika and the Haunted Hotel

Illustrated by Frank Rodgers

PUFFIN

For Clare and Kate who helped me with this one

PUFFIN BOOKS

Published by the Penguin Group
Penguin Books Ltd, 80 Strand, London WC2R 0RL, England
Penguin Group (USA) Inc., 375 Hudson Street, New York, New York 10014, USA
Penguin Group (Canada), 90 Eglinton Avenue East, Suite 700, Toronto, Ontario, Canada M4P 2Y3
(a division of Pearson Penguin Canada Inc.)
Penguin Ireland, 25 St Stephen's Green, Dublin 2, Ireland (a division of Penguin Books Ltd)
Penguin Group (Australia), 250 Camberwell Road, Camberwell,
Victoria 3124, Australia (a division of Pearson Australia Group Pty Ltd)
Penguin Books India Pvt Ltd, 11 Community Centre,
Panchsheel Park, New Delhi – 110 017, India
Penguin Group (NZ), cnr Airborne and Rosedale Roads, Albany,
Auckland 1310, New Zealand (a division of Pearson New Zealand Ltd)
Penguin Books (South Africa) (Pty) Ltd, 24 Sturdee Avenue,
Rosebank, Johannesburg 2196, South Africa

Penguin Books Ltd, Registered Offices: 80 Strand, London WC2R 0RL, England

www.penguin.com

First published by Viking Kestrel 1987
Published in Puffin Books 1988

001

This edition published 2006 for Index Books Ltd

Text copyright © Humphrey Carpenter, 1987
Illustrations copyright © Frank Rodgers, 1987
All rights reserved

The moral right of the author and illustrator has been asserted

Set in Palatino

Printed in England by Clays Ltd, St Ives plc

British Library Cataloguing in Publication Data
A CIP catalogue record for this book is available from the British Library

ISBN 978-0-14-134701-1

www.greenpenguin.co.uk

MIX
Paper from
responsible sources
FSC
www.fsc.org   FSC™ C018179

Penguin Books is committed to a sustainable
future for our business, our readers and our planet.
This book is made from Forest Stewardship
Council™ certified paper.

ALWAYS LEARNING   PEARSON

Contents

1. *The lollipop lady*

It was Monday morning at St Barty's School and, as usual, four people from Class Three were late.

Hamish Bigmore was late because he had overslept. This was because he had stayed up very late to watch a film on television. The film was called *The Deadly Slime*. At breakfast, Hamish upset his parents by pretending to be the Deadly Slime. He pretended to be the Deadly Slime all over the breakfast table. The Deadly Slime crawled all over the butter and the Corn Flakes and the milk jug until Mrs Bigmore came over faint, and Mr Bigmore hurried Hamish off to school.

Jody was late because she couldn't make up her mind which dress to wear, or should it be her dungarees, and which shirt went best with them? She changed her clothes six times before breakfast.

Thomas and Pete were late because Thomas couldn't find his right shoe, and Pete couldn't find his left shoe. In the end Thomas's right shoe was discovered inside Pete's left wellington boot, and Pete's left shoe was discovered on the right foot of Thomas's old teddy.

Hamish Bigmore, Jody, Thomas and Pete all came hurrying down the lane about five minutes after school had started. An old lady stepped out from behind a tree.

'Wait a minute, my little chicks!' she called. 'Auntie Mina will help you little toddlers across the road. She'll stop the dangerous cars and lorries from running into you.'

She was wearing a rather grubby looking

raincoat and hat, and was holding a traffic
sign shaped like a lollipop, with the word
STOP! painted on it.

'Dangerous cars and lorries?' laughed
Thomas. 'Don't be silly! The only thing that
ever comes down this lane is the Vicar on
his bicycle.'

'And anyway,' said Pete crossly, 'we're not
toddlers. We can look after ourselves.'

'Don't be rude,' whispered Jody. 'I'm

sure she means well, even if she is a bit cracked.'

Hamish Bigmore said nothing. He was having a careful look at the lollipop lady, as if he recognized her.

The old lady took their arms (Thomas noticed that she had a strong grip) and led them across the road. 'Thank you,' said Jody politely.

'Not at all, my little dears,' said the lollipop lady. 'Now, off you go to your playgroup, and have a lovely time in the sand-pit, and playing with your toys.'

'It isn't a playgroup,' said Thomas angrily. 'We're Class Three, and we're learning a lot of important things with our teacher, Mr Majeika. This term he's teaching us all about the Romans in Britain, and next week we're going on a trip to see Hadrian's Wall, which is a very old wall that a Roman Emperor built in the north of England.'

'Is that so, my little chick?' said the lollipop lady. 'Tell Auntie Mina all about it.'

'Ssh,' whispered Jody to Thomas. 'It's none of her business. Come on, we're late.' They hurried across the playground to Mr Majeika's classroom.

'Come back, little chickies,' called the lollipop lady. 'You didn't wait for one of Auntie Mina's lovely juicy sweets!'

'We never take sweets from strangers,' answered Pete.

'There's something peculiar about her,' said Jody. 'Don't you think so, Hamish?'

Hamish Bigmore shrugged his shoulders. 'She looked all right to me. Rather a nice old lady, in fact.'

Pete and Thomas looked at each other. It wasn't like Hamish Bigmore to say that somebody was nice.

*

At the end of the morning, Jody told Mr Majeika all about the lollipop lady. 'She certainly sounds odd,' he said. 'Let's go and take a look at her.'

But the lollipop lady had disappeared.

'I wonder . . .' said Mr Majeika. 'You say she was very interested in Class Three?'

Jody nodded.

'And she called herself "Auntie Mina"?'

'That's right,' said Jody.

'Well, what name does "Auntie Mina" remind you of?'

Jody thought for a moment. 'Wilhelmina Worlock! But you don't think . . .?'

Mr Majeika scratched his head. 'Well,' he said, 'I'm afraid it's possible.'

Wilhelmina Worlock was a music teacher who had come to St Barty's last term. She wasn't just a music teacher. She was a witch.

She had tried to take over the whole school, and she had made them spend their whole day playing in her orchestra. When people didn't obey her, she said she'd turn them into toads. The only person who had liked her was Hamish Bigmore. She called him her Star Pupil and said she would teach him magic. In the end, she had been stopped by Mr Majeika, who knew as much magic as she did. Mr Majeika had once been a wizard, though he didn't like people to know this, and he never wanted to do magic nowadays. But sometimes it was necessary, and he had used his magic to get rid of Wilhelmina Worlock.

'Do you really think it's her, come back?' asked Jody.

'I'm awfully afraid it may be,' said Mr Majeika. 'And if it is her, I'm sure she wants to get her revenge.'

Mr Potter, the headteacher of St Barty's, came strolling across the playground.

'Excuse me, Mr Potter,' said Mr Majeika, 'but have you seen an old lady helping children across the road outside school?'

'Certainly,' said Mr Potter. 'A very nice old lady. She took me across, and made sure the Vicar didn't bump into me on his bicycle.'

'She's been offering sweets to the children,' said Mr Majeika.

'Really?' said Mr Potter. 'Now you mention it, she gave me one. I quite forgot

15

to eat it.' He looked in his pocket, and found the sweet. He was about to pop it into his mouth when Mr Majeika snatched it from him.

'Don't eat it!' cried Mr Majeika.

He and Jody peered at the sweet. It was sticky and green, and was in the shape of a toad.

'Oh dear,' said Jody.

'Goodness,' said Mr Majeika. 'If Mr Potter had eaten this, he would have turned into a toad. Auntie Mina the lollipop lady is Wilhelmina Worlock, come to get her own back on Class Three. We shall all of us have to be very careful.'

2. Miss Worlock asks for help

Wilhelmina Worlock sat in a bus shelter, just around the corner from St Barty's. She was very cross indeed.

Her plan to turn Class Three into toads by giving them magic sweets had failed. She

had seen Mr Majeika coming to look for the lollipop lady, and she'd guessed that everyone had recognized her.

She fumed and muttered, but no other plan for revenge on Class Three would come into her head. It made her very cross.

In the old days, when she had been a young witch, surrounded by magical servants – genies and the like – she had been full of the nastiest ideas. Now her head was empty.

Wait a minute. Genies!

A thought crossed her horrid brain. There had been one particular genie she'd always found most useful. Jim the Genie was his name. He would do anything she asked, move whole mountains if necessary. He was as strong as the Genie of the Lamp in *Aladdin*.

Genies never die, so he must be around somewhere. She tried to remember how she used to summon him up. In *Aladdin* they rubbed a lamp to make the genie appear. But

Wilhelmina didn't think she'd used a lamp to call Jim the Genie.

Ah, now she remembered. She'd rubbed the end of her nose.

She tried it right away. At first nothing happened. Then she gave a terrific sneeze. Bother!

But the sneeze had done the trick. There was a puff of smoke which filled the bus shelter, so that Miss Worlock coughed and spluttered.

'Yes, Madam?' said a voice. 'Can I fetch you anything?'

A tall man in a black suit was standing there. He had a cloth folded neatly over one arm, and a tray tucked under the other. Miss Worlock could see that he was a waiter.

'Who are you?' she screamed. 'I want Jim the Genie.'

'Madam,' said the waiter politely, 'I *am* James the Genie. And you, Madam, unless I am much mistaken, are Miss W. Worlock,

whom I had the pleasure of serving many years ago. May I get you something, Madam?'

'Thank you, James,' said Miss Worlock. 'I'll have a large sherry, with an eye of newt floating on the top. No, what am I talking about? I don't want a drink! It wasn't a *waiter* I called for. Have you given up being a genie?'

Jim the Genie bowed low. 'Well, Madam,

as I grew older, I felt I should take an easier job. I have opened a hotel.'

'A *hotel*?' screamed Miss Worlock. 'What do I want to know about *hotels*?'

'If I may say so, Madam,' continued Jim the Genie, 'it is a very good hotel. Allow me to show you our card.' He handed it to Miss Worlock:

THE GREEN BANANA HOTEL
Wobbleswick, near Hadrian's Wall
Comfortable rooms, excellent cooking
Proprietor: J. Genie, Esq.

Miss Worlock tore it into pieces. 'Stop wasting my time!' she shouted. 'Can't you still do any magic?'

Jim the Genie bowed low. 'Madam, once a genie, always a genie.'

'Then get on with it!' shrieked Miss Worlock. 'I want you to turn the school upside down.'

'Madam?' asked Jim the Genie, with a puzzled frown.

'The *school*, you idiot! That one over there, St Botty's or whatever they call it. Turn it upside down, and give them the biggest fright of their lives!'

Jim the Genie bowed low. 'Your wish, Madam, is my command.'

*

Thomas, Pete and Jody were going home

past the bus shelter when they heard a frightful noise.

They all looked into the shelter. A tall man, dressed as a waiter, was holding Miss Worlock upside down. He was grasping her by the heels, and shaking her hard.

'Is that enough, Madam?' he was asking her.

'It's not working,' screamed Miss Worlock. 'The school has turned upside down, I can see that, but no one's falling out of it.'

Thomas, Pete and Jody started to giggle. Miss Worlock saw them.

'You've cheated me!' she roared at Jim the Genie. 'It's not the school that's upside down, it's *me!*'

Jody, Pete and Thomas ran away, though they were laughing so much it was hard to run.

'I do beg your pardon, Madam,' said Jim the Genie to Miss Worlock, 'but it occurred to me that if *you* were upside down, it might serve just as well.'

'I'll turn you into a toad!' shrieked Miss Worlock. 'I suppose you were too old and feeble to lift the school in the air? Get back to your hotel! I can see you're no longer any use as a genie. Get back to your silly hotel, and –'

She paused. She had an idea.

'James,' she said thoughtfully, 'this hotel of yours. It's near Hadrian's Wall?'

Jim the Genie bowed low. 'It is, Madam.'

'*Aha*,' said Miss Worlock.

3. Hamish and the Romans

Hamish Bigmore was making a great nuisance of himself about the visit to Hadrian's Wall. 'Romans!' he kept on sneering. 'Who wants to hear about silly old Romans? What's supposed to be so clever about them?'

'Well,' said Jody, 'they invented a language called Latin, and they made coins, and they built big houses with hot baths and central heating.'

'Latin!' laughed Hamish Bigmore. 'Coins, hot baths. What's so clever about *that*? I bet *I* could make up a language, and as for hot baths and central heating, my Mum and Dad have got *those* at home! If you ask me, the

Romans were just a lot of silly savages, walking about in old sheets.'

'They built Hadrian's Wall,' said Jody.

'Hadrian's Wall!' laughed Hamish. 'Why, even my dad can build a *wall*. He's just put one up to keep the neighbour's dog out of our garden. I suppose in a hundred years' time people will be coming on expeditions to see Mr Bigmore's Wall!'

'Don't be an idiot,' said Jody.

'You tell me one thing,' said Hamish. 'Had the Romans got guns? Had they got televisions? Had they got computers?'

'No,' said Jody.

'Then that proves it,' said Hamish. 'We're cleverer than they were. So what's the point of going to see their silly old wall?'

The day before the expedition, Class Three performed a play about the Romans in Britain, with the rest of the school watching. Mr Majeika had rehearsed them in their parts. Thomas and Pete were two Roman soldiers called Tiberius and Petrus, and there was a scene where they captured a British tribe, and made them all Roman citizens.

Hamish Bigmore was supposed to be one of the British tribe who got captured, but up to the last minute he refused to have anything to do with it. He just sat in a corner sulking, while they rehearsed. Then suddenly he changed his mind. 'I bet he's up to something,' said Pete.

Sure enough, when they got to the scene where Tiberius and Petrus capture the British tribe, Hamish Bigmore ran on to the stage and pulled a toy machine-gun from under his British costume. 'Stick 'em up, you guys!' he roared. 'This is Hamishus Bigmorus, the only Ancient Briton who knew anything about guns. Stick 'em up, or I'll plug you all full of lead!'

Thomas and Pete tried to carry on, but Melanie, who was playing a Roman lady, burst into tears and ran off the stage. Mr

Majeika had to make them begin it all again,
after Hamish Bigmore had been sent home.
'I'd like to punish Hamish by saying he can't
come on the expedition to Hadrian's Wall,'
said Mr Majeika. 'But since he doesn't want
to come anyway, it wouldn't really be a
punishment.'

*

The next morning, the bus was waiting
outside the school gates. Hamish didn't
appear until it was time to go. Class Three
had hoped he wouldn't turn up at all. But
just as the bus was starting, he walked
cheerfully up to it, whistling brightly, and
carrying a piece of paper.

'So you *are* coming with us?' asked Mr
Majeika.

'Oh yes,' said Hamish. 'I wouldn't miss it
for anything. Good old Hadrian's Wall!'

'On the bus, everyone,' called Mr Potter,
who was coming with them. Hamish found
a seat just in front of Thomas and Pete.

'What's that bit of paper?' asked Thomas.

'None of *your* business,' said Hamish.

The bus got going, and Thomas and Pete, peering between the seats, saw Hamish unfold the paper. On it was written, in straggly, spidery handwriting:

To my Star Pupil!
Don't forget to get on the bus to Hadrian's Wall.
You can help me get my revenge on them all!
See you at the Green Banana!

W. W.

'I can guess who it's from,' whispered Thomas, 'but what does it mean about a green banana?'

Pete shook his head. 'I don't know. But I don't like the look of it.'

*

It was a very long journey to Hadrian's Wall, and the driver had to keep stopping for Melanie to be sick. When they got to a town for lunch, it took them ages to get

going again, because Pandora and her friends
William and Clare and Kate had disappeared.
Mr Majeika found them in a video shop
watching cartoons. And then Mr Potter
disappeared too, and it turned out that he
had got on the wrong bus, with a
completely different lot of children from
another school. By the time they were on
their way again, it was starting to get
dark, and Mr Majeika was worried that

they wouldn't reach Hadrian's Wall before night, though he'd told the place where they were to stay that they'd arrive by tea-time.

They drove up on to the moors, and it became very foggy, and the bus had to go slower and slower because the driver couldn't see properly. Mr Majeika kept looking anxiously at his watch.

'Oh dear,' he said. 'Well, I suppose we'll get there in the end.'

Just at that moment, the bus began to bump dreadfully, and shake about from side to side. Then it stopped altogether. The driver got out.

'Flat tyres,' he said.

'Oh dear,' said Mr Majeika. 'But you can mend it, can't you?'

'It's not just one,' said the driver. 'Every single tyre is flat. There's a whole lot of drawing-pins across the road. Someone's done it on purpose. I'll have to ring up a garage.'

'Bother,' said Mr Majeika. 'And everyone is very tired and hungry.'

'Couldn't you magic us some food, Mr Magic?' said Pandora.

Mr Majeika shook his head. 'Certainly not. You know I never use magic if I can possibly help it.'

'There's no need to worry,' said Hamish Bigmore, who had been peering through the window. 'We've broken down just outside a hotel.'

'A hotel?' said Mr Majeika. 'That will be frightfully expensive.'

'Oh, I shouldn't think so,' said Hamish. 'It looks pretty cheap. It's called the Green Banana.'

4. *The Green Banana*

'The Green Banana!' whispered Thomas to Pete.

Mr Potter was getting out of the bus. 'I shall go and ask the hotel if they have food for everyone,' he said. 'I'll be back in a few minutes.'

'I think I'll go and help him,' said Hamish Bigmore, and slipped out of the bus.

They all waited, and nobody came back.

Mr Majeika began to look worried. The driver had disappeared some time ago, to telephone a garage. It was very dark and foggy.

After a while, Jody said: 'Oughtn't we to go and see what's happening?'

Mr Majeika shook his head. 'I think we should all stay safely on the bus.'

'There's something peculiar going on,' said Pete. 'Hamish Bigmore seemed to know all about the Green Banana before we arrived here.'

'In that case,' said Mr Majeika, 'we should certainly stay where we are. It's much safer here.'

Melanie began to cry. 'I want to go home!'

While Mr Majeika did his best to comfort her, Jody, Thomas and Pete slipped out of the bus. 'I want to find out what's going on,' whispered Thomas.

'Quite right,' said Jody. 'If Hamish Bigmore is up to some trick, we should.try and stop him.'

It was very dark, and the fog was so thick that they could only just see the Green Banana Hotel. There was no light in any of the windows. 'I don't like the look of it at all,' whispered Pete.

They reached the door, and pushed it open.
It made a creaking noise: *crrrreeeeaaaak.* Inside,
the entrance hall was dimly lit. They looked
all around them, but there was no sign of
Mr Potter or Hamish. Everything was very
quiet.

Suddenly they heard somebody say
something in the back part of the building.
It sounded like 'Help!'

They all looked at each other. 'I think,' said Thomas, 'that I want to go back to the bus.'

'Me too,' said Pete.

'Oh, don't be cowards,' said Jody. 'I'm sure it's perfectly safe, though it *is* a bit like those Ghost Trains they have at fairs, where everything is very dark, and then nasty things jump out at you.'

'Talking of fairs,' said Pete, 'look! There's one of those machines that takes your photograph, and prints it while you wait. I've always wanted to try that.'

'Me too,' said Thomas.

'Oh, don't waste time,' said Jody. But the boys had already clambered into the machine and put in their money. They grinned at the camera while the light flashed.

'Hurray,' said Pete. 'Now all we have to do is wait for the picture. It'll drop out of the machine in a few minutes.'

There was another noise from somewhere. This time it was a sort of rattling.

'Oh dear,' said Thomas. 'It sounds a bit like chains. The sort that ghosts clank about in.'

'Yes,' said Pete. 'Or perhaps the bones of a skeleton rattling. Let's go back to the bus.'

'Oh, come on,' said Jody. Unwillingly, the boys followed her.

They found themselves in a long dark passage. At the end of it was a greenish light. Holding their breath, they tiptoed down the passage, feeling in front of them in case there were spiders' webs or other nasty things that come and tickle you in Ghost Trains.

The light was coming from a glass door at the end of the passage. 'Look,' whispered Jody, pointing at a notice. 'It's the Dining Room.'

'Oh,' said Pete, 'I thought it said "Dying Room".'

The glass door was all crinkly, and they

could not see through it, but Thomas found
a keyhole, and peered through that.

He went very white. 'Oh no!' he said.

'What's the matter?' whispered Pete. He
had a turn at looking, and went pale. 'It's
ghastly!' he whispered.

'What is it?' whispered Jody.

'It's some sort of ogre,' answered Pete.
'Like in stories. The kind that catch children,
and cook and eat them.'

40

'He looks quite ghastly,' whispered Thomas. 'He's sitting at a table, eating something out of a bowl. His eyes are all sunken, and he's got this ugly great mouth, and a huge bald head with wisps of hair sticking out.'

'Let me see,' said Jody, shuddering. 'He sounds terrible.'

She peered through the keyhole. Then she said: 'You idiots, it's Mr Potter!'

They opened the dining-room door. Mr Potter was sitting at a table under a green lampshade, finishing a bowl of soup.

'That tasted very good,' he said. 'We should certainly have supper here, and stay the night. I thought I'd better try some of the food before we decided.'

'Did you call out "help"?' asked Jody.

Mr Potter shook his head. 'I was asking the waiter for a second helping.'

'I suppose what we thought was chains or a skeleton was Mr Potter's spoon clinking,' said Thomas. 'We've been idiots. Come on, let's go back to the bus.'

They all went down the passage. 'We thought you were an ogre,' Jody said to Mr Potter.

'Yes,' said Pete, 'and we thought the hotel was haunted. We were quite sure it was full of horrible ghosts.'

Suddenly Jody screamed. 'It *is* haunted. Look at those ghastly faces!'

She pointed at the carpet. Two ghoulish faces were grinning up at them.

Mr Potter bent down. 'Quite a good likeness,' he said to Thomas and Pete. It was their photograph, which had fallen out of the machine on to the carpet.

'You idiots!' said Jody. 'Your photo looks like the ugliest ghosts in the world.'

'Well,' said Thomas, 'it seems as though there aren't any spooks around after all. This is just an ordinary hotel.'

But when they got back to the bus, Mr Majeika and Class Three had vanished.

5. Send for the police

'Oh dear, whatever shall we do?' said Jody.

'I think we had better send for the police,' said Mr Potter. 'You telephone, and I'll go on searching.' He went out.

There was a telephone in the corner. Pete dialled 999. 'I want the police station,' he said.

A voice answered: 'Wobbleswick Police Station. P.C. Buttonbottom speaking.'

'P.C. *who*?' said Pete.

'P.C. Buttonbottom,' said the voice. 'And don't you laugh at my name, young fellow, or I'll have you arrested for being rude to the police.'

This didn't sound like the sort of

policeman who was going to be much use.
Pete said: 'I'm speaking from the Green
Banana Hotel.'

'*Aha*,' said P.C. Buttonbottom, 'the Green
Banana Hotel.'

'Why did you say "*Aha*"?' asked Pete.

'Why shouldn't I say "*Aha*"?' answered
P.C. Buttonbottom. 'I can say "fiddlesticks",
or "raspberry yoghurt", or "stick a chicken
up your nose" if I want to. I'm a policeman.
I can do anything I like.'

'I think he's a bit potty,' Pete whispered to Jody. 'You have a go.'

'Hallo,' said Jody into the telephone.

'Oh, it's you, Jody, is it?' said P.C. Buttonbottom.

Jody was amazed. 'How did you know my name?' she asked.

'Something very peculiar is going on,' Thomas said to Pete.

'We're at the Green Banana Hotel,' said Jody into the telephone, 'and a lot of children and a teacher have disappeared. Will you please come up here and help us find them?'

'Of course,' said P.C. Buttonbottom, and rang off. A moment later, a door opened, and out stepped someone in a policeman's uniform.

'I'm P.C. Buttonbottom of the Wobbleswick Constabulary,' he said.

He was no taller than Thomas, Pete, or Jody, and there was something familiar about

him, though Pete couldn't think what it was.
A large beard and moustache covered his face.

'How did you come so fast, in a car or
on a bike?' asked Jody.

P.C. Buttonbottom didn't answer.

'There's a lot of children missing,' said
Jody.

'Aha,' said P.C. Buttonbottom. 'What are
they missing? Their shoes and socks? I missed
a bus last week.'

'Don't be silly,' said Pete. 'We mean they've vanished, disappeared.'

'Aha,' said P.C. Buttonbottom, 'I recognize your voice. You're the one who was rude to me on the telephone. I can put you in prison for a thousand years.'

'He can't be a real policeman,' whispered Jody.

Thomas said: 'Please will you help us find the missing children, and Mr Majeika. We need to look everywhere.'

'What a good idea,' said P.C. Buttonbottom. 'What a clever policeman you'd make, my lad. Look everywhere! Oh yes, let's look everywhere. You try under the carpet and I'll look in all the drawers.' And P.C. Buttonbottom burst out laughing.

'I know that laugh,' said Jody, and she made a grab for P.C. Buttonbottom. But he disappeared through a door, slammed it after him, and locked it.

'Who was it?' Thomas asked.

'Didn't you recognize him?' said Jody.

At that moment, Mr Potter came back. 'I can't find the others anywhere,' he said.

'We fetched a policeman,' said Jody, 'but he turned out not to be a real one. Even if this hotel isn't haunted, there's something very funny going on. You'll never guess who the policeman really was.'

The door through which P.C. Buttonbottom had vanished suddenly opened, and there was a ghostly noise. Something dressed all in white was standing in the doorway.

'I don't like this,' said Thomas.

'Goodness,' said Mr Potter, 'it's an Ancient Roman.'

Indeed, the figure that now came through the door was dressed in what looked like a Roman toga, a sort of white sheet wound around its body. On its head was a crown made of leaves. Like P.C. Buttonbottom, it had a beard and moustache.

'W-w-w-who are y-y-y-you?' said Mr Potter.

'I,' said the figure in a ghostly voice, 'am the Emperor Hadrian.'

'D-d-do you really think it is?' whispered Thomas. His teeth were chattering.

'Well, if it is,' said Pete, 'the Emperor Hadrian looks awfully like P.C. Buttonbottom.'

'I am the Emperor Hadrian,' said the ghost. 'It was me that built Hadrian's Wall.'

'How very interesting,' said Mr Potter, who seemed to believe that the ghost was real. 'Do tell me why you built it.'

'I built the Wall,' said the ghost, 'because the fence had fallen down.' He started to giggle.

'They tell us in the history books,' said Mr Potter, 'that you built the Wall to keep out the Picts and the Scots. What sort of people were they?'

'Well,' said the ghost of the Emperor Hadrian, 'the Picts were called Picts because they were always picking their noses. And you could tell them from the Scots, because the Scots were always wiping their noses on their kilts.'

Mr Potter scratched his head. 'I see,' he

said. 'I suppose it was very cold on the Wall?'

'Oh yes,' said the Emperor Hadrian. 'Mind you, I was never *on* the Wall for very long. I kept falling off it! And it was much warmer in my house.'

'In your house?' asked Mr Potter.

'Oh yes,' said the Emperor Hadrian. 'All our houses had hot baths and central heating. And *I* was cleverer than all the other Ancient Romans, so I had a television and a computer, and lots and lots of guns!'

'It isn't a ghost,' shouted Thomas. *'It's Hamish Bigmore!!'*

'Of course it is,' said Jody. 'And he was P.C. Buttonbottom too. Get him!'

The Emperor Hadrian tried to escape through the door, but this time they were too quick for him. He was still wearing the policeman costume under the Roman toga. The beard and moustache were stuck on with glue, and he yelled when they pulled them off.

'Where did you get these clothes and things?' asked Jody.

'Shan't tell you,' said Hamish Bigmore.

'And where are all the others, and Mr Majeika?' said Pete.

'Shan't tell you,' said Hamish Bigmore.

'Tickle him,' said Jody.

Thomas and Pete tickled him while Jody held his arms. 'Help!' spluttered Hamish. 'All

53

right, I'll tell you. But it won't do you, or them, any good at all.' And he laughed very nastily.

6. *Miss Worlock meets Miss Worlock*

Thomas, Pete, Jody and Mr Potter followed Hamish Bigmore into the hotel kitchen. On the far side was a door labelled COLD STORAGE. 'In there,' said Hamish sulkily.

Thomas opened the door. Inside were Mr Majeika and Class Three. Mr Majeika looked rather cold, but the rest of them seemed happy enough.

'However did you get in there?' asked Jody.

'Hamish Bigmore did it,' said Mr Majeika. 'He came to the bus and said that dinner was ready, and he brought us here and shut us in. I ought to have known better than to follow him.'

'And didn't you get any dinner?' asked Thomas.

'No,' said Mr Majeika. 'But there's a big box of ice creams in the corner, and we've all been eating our way through them.'

'They're yummy,' said Pandora, licking her lips.

'I've eaten too many,' said Melanie. 'I feel sick.'

56

'Why didn't you use your magic to let everyone out?' asked Pete.

'I tried to think of something,' said Mr Majeika. 'I thought I might manage to summon up a magic carpet, or perhaps make us all grow tiny, so that we could crawl out through the keyhole. But no one would let me do anything till they'd finished the ice creams. They were enjoying them so much.'

'Well, tell them to hurry up,' said Jody, 'and then we can all go home. I'm sure the bus tyres are mended by now.'

'Tee hee!' said a voice behind her. 'Tee hee! How nice to see you all again. And welcome to the Green Banana Hotel!'

'Oh dear,' said Mr Majeika. 'I rather guessed that *you* were behind this, Wilhelmina Worlock. ' Miss Worlock was standing there, rubbing her hands.

'Was it you that dressed up Hamish as a

policeman, and as the Emperor Hadrian?'
asked Jody.

'Of course, dearie,' said Miss Worlock.
'My Star Pupil deserved his little bit of fun,
in return for bringing you all here. And now
that you *are* here, you're all going to sign
up for the Wilhelmina Worlock School of
Music. I've got a piece of paper which says
that Class Three of St Barty's School agree
to be my pupils, and mine alone. You're
going to give up all other classwork,
and learn music from Wilhelmina all day
long.'

'Are you going to keep us all here as
prisoners?' asked Thomas.

'Oh no, dearie, not if you sign the paper.
You can go back to St Barty's, only it won't
be called St Barty's any more. It'll be the
Wilhelmina Worlock School of Music, tee
hee!'

'Tee hee,' said Hamish Bigmore.

Jody kicked him on the ankle.

'I'll turn you into a toad,' hissed Hamish. '*She*'ll show me how.'

'And do you really expect us to agree to this?' asked Mr Majeika.

'Oh yes, dearie,' answered Miss Worlock. 'Because if you don't sign the paper, it's back in the cold storage with you all. And this time there won't be any ice-cream to eat. A horrible headless waiter will serve you with stewed worms and boiled snakes, and you'll be sitting in the cold and the dark, and in the end you'll be screaming to be let out, and you'll sign the paper, just like that.'

'A h-h-headless w-w-waiter?' asked Melanie.

'Yes, dearie,' said Miss Worlock. She gave the piece of paper to Mr Potter. 'You're in charge of them all, so you sign it first.'

Mr Potter felt in his pocket. 'I seem to have lost my pen,' he said.

'You can use mine,' said Miss Worlock. Suddenly she dropped it with a yell. It had turned into a red-hot poker.

'Oho,' she said to Mr Majeika, 'up to your old tricks again?'

Mr Majeika smiled. 'Why blame me? Really, Wilhelmina, you should get a better pen.'

'Of course it was him!' said Hamish Bigmore. 'He turned my ruler into a snake, the very first day he came and taught Class

Three. Here's another pen.' He gave one to
Mr Potter.

Mr Potter took it, and started to sign the
paper. This time the pen turned into a yo-
yo.

'Goodness,' said Mr Potter. 'What's this?'

'It's called a yo-yo,' said Jody. 'I'll show
you how it works.'

Mr Potter started to play with the yo-yo.

'That's enough of that!' shrieked Miss

Worlock. She found a pencil, and gave it to Mr Potter. 'Sign, you nincompoop!'

Mr Potter started to write, but before he had finished, he was yawning. 'Oh dear,' he said, 'I've come over all sleepy. I don't think I've done it quite right.'

Miss Worlock grabbed the paper and looked at it. 'No, you haven't, you blithering idiot! You haven't written your name at all. You've written "I'm Popeye the Sailor Man".'

'Oh, so sorry,' said Mr Potter. 'It's been such a long day, I don't know what's got into my brain.'

'*I* know what's got into your brain all right,' snapped Miss Worlock. She turned to Mr Majeika. 'It's *you*, isn't it? You've hypnotized him into writing rubbish, you interfering little man! Behave yourself, or I'll turn you into an ice-cream, and your own class can gobble you up.'

In response, Mr Majeika turned himself into a jelly.

It was a very big, very red, very wobbly jelly. They knew it was Mr Majeika because it had his face.

'Oh, *I* see, dearie,' snarled Miss Worlock. 'You want to play *that* little game again. Haven't you realized that I can beat you at *that* any day?' And she turned herself into a giant spoon.

The spoon (which had Miss Worlock's face) advanced on the jelly. Clearly it was

going to spoon it all up, though Class Three knew that, just in time, Mr Majeika would manage to turn himself into something else. They'd seen him and Miss Worlock do this sort of thing before.

So had Hamish Bigmore. 'Stop!' he cried, to the Miss Worlock spoon. 'I've got a better idea!' He whispered something to it.

The spoon stopped being a spoon, and turned into Mr Majeika.

'Well, *that's* all right,' said Thomas happily.

'What a near thing, Mr Majeika. But what's happened to Miss Worlock?'

'I don't know,' said Mr Majeika. 'Perhaps she's got stuck as something she turned herself into. Never mind, let's get out of here and back to the bus.'

Everyone cheered, until Jody stopped them. 'Excuse me,' she said to Mr Majeika, 'but *you* were the spoon just now. And before the spoon became a spoon, it was Miss Worlock. So how do we know you're really Mr Majeika?'

'Oh, don't be silly, dearie,' said Mr Majeika.

That didn't sound like Mr Majeika, even if it looked like him. Class Three looked anxiously at each other.

'Well done, Jody,' said a voice. 'I thought for a moment she'd fooled you.'

The jelly had turned into another Mr Majeika.

'*You*'re the real one, aren't you?' Pete said to him.

'Of course I am,' he said.

'Of course he's not,' said the other Mr Majeika.

Class Three looked from one Mr Majeika to the other. There was no way of telling which was the real one. They were both the same from top to toe.

'Now, come along with me,' said the first Mr Majeika, the one who had been the spoon, the one who must really be Miss Worlock.

'No, come along with *me*,' said the second one, the one who had been the jelly. At least, they *thought* he was the one who had been the jelly. Already it was getting difficult to remember.

'You idiots,' sneered Hamish Bigmore. 'You haven't the faintest idea which is which. You can't even remember that *this* one was Mr Majeika to start with, and *this* one was Miss Worlock. Or was it the other way round? Let's try and guess. We could toss a coin for it. Or play eenie meenie.'

'Oh, do shut up, Hamish,' said Thomas.
'You've muddled everyone.'

'I've got an idea,' called out Pandora. 'If
the real Mr Majeika would turn himself into
something else, it would have his face on it,
or her face if it was really Miss Worlock, and
then we'd know which was which.'

'All right,' said the first Mr Majeika.

'All right,' said the second Mr Majeika.
And they both turned into something else.

In fact they both turned into Miss Worlock.

'Tee hee!' said the first Miss Worlock.

'Tee hee!' said the second Miss Worlock.

'Oh dear,' said Jody, 'this is worse than ever.'

7. A visit to Rome

'Well now,' said one of the Miss Worlocks to Hamish Bigmore, 'you're my Star Pupil, go and find me another pencil so that I can make Mr Potter sign that piece of paper, tee hee!'

'Very clever,' sneered the other Miss Worlock. 'You may *look* just like me, dearie, but you can't do half the things the real Wilhelmina Worlock can.'

'Such as, dearie?' asked the first Miss Worlock.

The second Miss Worlock thought for a moment. Then she said: 'I bet you can't turn Hamish Bigmore into a toad.'

'Of course I can,' said the first Miss Worlock. 'I bet it's *you* that can't!'

'Of course I can,' said the second. 'Look, I'll show you.'

'So will I,' said the other.

'No!' yelled Hamish. 'Stop it! I've been your favourite pupil, at least for one of you, whichever it is. Don't treat me like this!' He got on his knees in front of one of the Miss Worlocks.

'That's the wrong one!' screeched the other. 'She's really *him*! *I'm me*!'

'Don't be fooled by *her*!' screeched the first Miss Worlock. 'Anyone can see that *I'm* the real Wilhelmina!'

'No you're not!' screamed the other.

'Yes I am!'

'No you're not!'

The first picked up a bag of flour, and burst it over the second. The second picked up a bowl of mashed potato, and emptied it over the first.

'Ladies, please!' said a voice. 'A little less noise, if you don't mind. I don't like such

70

squabbles going on in my hotel.'

It was Jim the Genie.

'*Your* hotel?' asked Jody, puzzled. 'You mean it doesn't belong to Miss Worlock?'

'Oh no, Miss,' answered Jim. 'The lady (and I see that at the moment there are two of her) borrowed it for the night, so as (I fear) to play some trick on you young people.'

'You mean it really isn't a haunted hotel?' asked Thomas.

'No, young sir. The Green Banana is an extremely respectable establishment.'

'No ghosts?' asked Pete.

'No, sir, no ghosts.'

'Will you be quiet!' shrieked one of the Miss Worlocks. 'There may be no ghosts, but there's *you*, a real live genie. Why don't you show them what genies can really do?'

'Don't talk rubbish,' screeched the other Miss Worlock. 'Anyone can see old Jim is far too old to be a working genie. He's lost all his magic powers, haven't you, Jim?'

Jim drew himself up to his full height. 'No, Madam, I have not.'

'Well then,' said the first Miss Worlock, 'kindly transport this hotel through the air, back in time, and across the world, to Ancient Rome, in the days of the Caesars – to the Colosseum!'

Jim raised his eyebrows. 'The Colosseum,

Madam? The big arena of Ancient Rome? Are you certain?'

'There you are,' screeched the other Miss Worlock. 'I told you. He's too old to do it!'

Jim looked upset. 'Certainly not, Madam. But Madam, do you know the sort of thing that went on in the Colosseum?'

'Of course!' screeched the first Miss Worlock. 'And since these kiddies are interested in all that old Roman rubbish, they might as well see it for themselves.'

'Your wish, Madam,' said Jim grandly, 'is my command.' He vanished in a cloud of smoke.

There was a deep rumbling sound, and Class Three felt the building begin to tremble. Everyone held on as the Green Banana Hotel started to rise up in the air.

A moment later they had bumped down on to land again.

'Don't you believe it!' screeched one of

the Miss Worlocks. 'He hasn't really done it. It's just a trick.'

Jim appeared again. 'We have arrived in Ancient Rome, Madam.'

'Thank you, James,' said the Miss Worlock who had asked him to do it. 'Let's all go and see.'

They trooped out to the front door of the hotel. Jim opened the door. 'Here you are, Madam,' he said. 'The Colosseum in the days of Ancient Rome.'

Spread in front of them, outside the door, was a huge amphitheatre. A gigantic crowd, thousands and thousands of Romans, were cheering the games that were in progress. Two teams of gladiators were fighting each other with swords.

'Well, dearie,' said the Miss Worlock who hadn't believed Jim could do it, 'that's all very clever, and now we can go home.'

At that moment a loud voice bellowed: 'By the order of the Emperor, the gladiator

games are now ended. It is time for a slave to be thrown to the lions!' The crowd cheered.

'Did you hear what I said, Jim?' snapped the same Miss Worlock. 'It's time to go home!'

'Not so fast, dearie,' said the other Miss Worlock. 'I think they're looking for you.'

'By the order of the Emperor,' shouted the

voice again, 'a slave shall be taken from the strange house that has magically appeared in our midst! The Emperor bids his soldiers go in there and fetch out a slave, to be thrown to the lions.'

'Jim!' shrieked the Miss Worlock who was getting frightened. 'Take us home!'

But it was too late. Two burly Romans, with spears and shields, stood in the doorway of the hotel. 'Slave!' they called to the frightened Miss Worlock. 'Come with us!'

'N-n-n-not today, thank you,' spluttered Miss Worlock.

'By order of the Emperor!' roared the soldiers. They put their hands under Miss Worlock's arms and carried her out into the arena, struggling and kicking.

'And now,' bellowed the voice, 'by order of the Emperor, release the lions!'

'No!' screeched Miss Worlock, and ran off like streaked lightning, vanishing into the

crowd as the soldiers gave chase after her.

'I think,' said Mr Majeika, turning back into himself – and Class Three was relieved to see that *he* had been the Miss Worlock who was *not* being chased through the Colosseum – 'I think that now it really *is* time to go home, before they come looking for another slave. James, would you please be so kind as to take us and the hotel back where we all belong?'

'Certainly, sir,' said Jim the Genie, and in a moment the Green Banana was safely in its usual place in England.

'Well,' said Mr Majeika, 'that should take care of Wilhelmina Worlock for a while! And now, would you mind, James, if we all stayed the night in your hotel? It's getting very late, and we need plenty of sleep if we are going to enjoy Hadrian's Wall tomorrow.'

'Of course, sir,' said Jim. 'Please be my

guests, and may I wish you all a pleasant night's rest?'

Hamish Bigmore crawled out from under the sofa, where he had been hiding since they went to Rome. 'Don't pay any attention!' he shouted. 'How do you know he's the real Mr Majeika? I bet you this is really Miss Worlock.'

'Well,' said Mr Majeika, 'how do we know that you're really Hamish Bigmore?'

'Of course I am,' shouted Hamish.

'Oh, are you?' answered another Hamish Bigmore. Mr Majeika had turned into an exact copy of him.

The real Hamish got very red in the face. 'Stop it!' he yelled. 'I'm me! You're just a pretend one!'

'How do you know?' said the pretend Hamish. 'Nobody can tell the difference. Yah boo sucks!' And he stuck out his tongue and made a rude noise at the first one.

'Stop it! Stop it!' shouted the real Hamish.

Mr Majeika had already stopped it. He was back in his own shape.

'I think even Hamish must be ready for bed after that,' he said. 'Good-night, everyone.'

'Good-night, Mr Majeika,' said Jody. 'And please, don't do that again. *One* Hamish Bigmore is quite enough. *Two*, well, it's more than anyone can stand!'